I Dreamed I was a Puppy Dog

Debra A. Johnson

Illustrated
by
Stephanie Kranz

Published by Abdo & Daughters, 4940 Viking Drive, Suite 622, Edina, Minnesota 55435.

Library bound edition distributed by Rockbottom Books, Pentagon Tower, P.O. Box 36036, Minneapolis, Minnesota 55435.

Printed in the United States.

Illustrations by Stephanie Kranz

Edited by Julie Berg

LIBRARY OF CONGRESS CATALOGING-IN-PUBLICATION DATA

Johnson, Debra A., 1961-
    I Dreamed I was--A Puppy Dog / Debra A. Johnson.
        p.   cm. -- (I Dreamed I was--)
    Summary: A child dreams of being a puppy and meeting some of the animals found in the United States.
    ISBN 1-56239-303-0
    [1. Dogs--Fiction. 2. Animals--Fiction. 3.Dreams--fiction. 4. Stories in rhyme.]
    I. Title. II. Title: Puppy Dog. III. Series: Johnson, Debra A., 1961-
    I Dreamed I was--
    PZ8.3.J6317Iap   1994
    [E]--dc20   94-15038
                                                                      CIP
                                                                      AC

I Dreamed I was a Puppy Dog

Debra A. Johnson

One day when I came home from school
I had nothing fun to do.
Toys and games were boring.
I wanted something new.
Then Mom gave me a picture
of a mountain by a stream.
She said, "Use this as a starting place
and draw yourself a dream."

I closed my eyes and wondered,
"What would walk these fields of green?"
Before long I was sleeping
and this is what I dreamed.

I dreamed I was a puppy dog
roaming wild and free.
There was a giant eagle
playing tag along with me.

**I must be in America
where the great bald eagles fly—
'cause that's a great bald eagle
that's soaring through the sky.**

I followed my new friend
across the grassy plains.
It showed me many animals
and told me all their names.

First we met some buffalo
and joined in their stampede.
I couldn't believe those big animals
could run with so much speed.

I thought I saw a weasel
chasing something like a mole.
But it was a black-footed ferret
who chased a prairie dog down a hole.

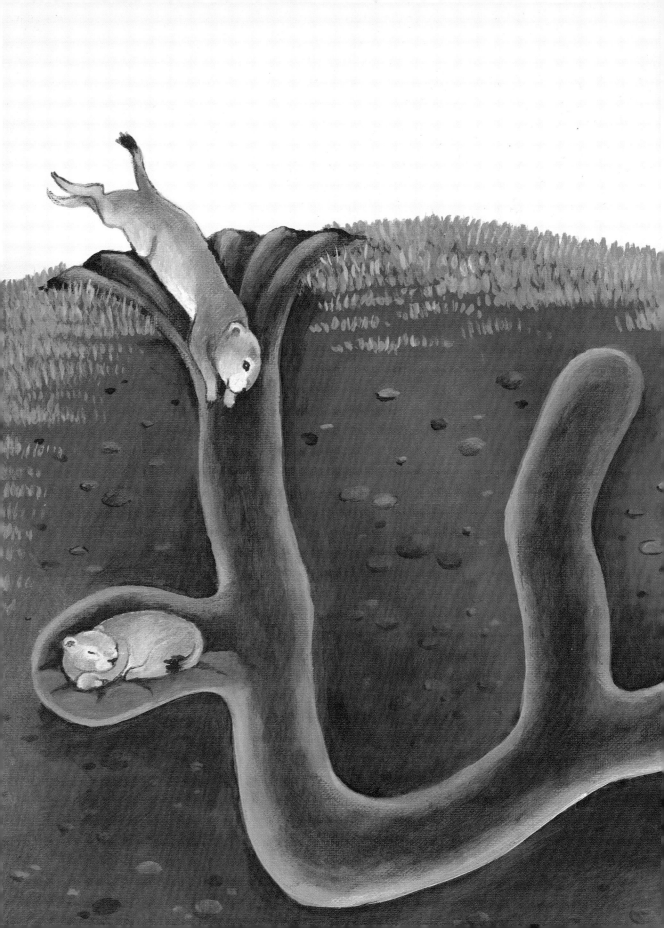

I saw what looked like a hunting dog
that made a scary sound.
The coyote's eerie howling
can be heard for miles around.

A porcupine's an animal
with prickly quills inside its fur.
She will poke them into creatures
if they try to frighten her.

Bobcats have long cheek ruffs
(that's sort of like a beard!).
They like to climb on hillsides
and by rabbits they are feared.

Beavers have sharp teeth they use
to chop down tall, thin trees.
Their tail is like a paddle
and it helps them swim with ease.

Gophers can carry a lot of food
in pouches in their cheeks.
They bring it to their nests
so they can hide down there for weeks.

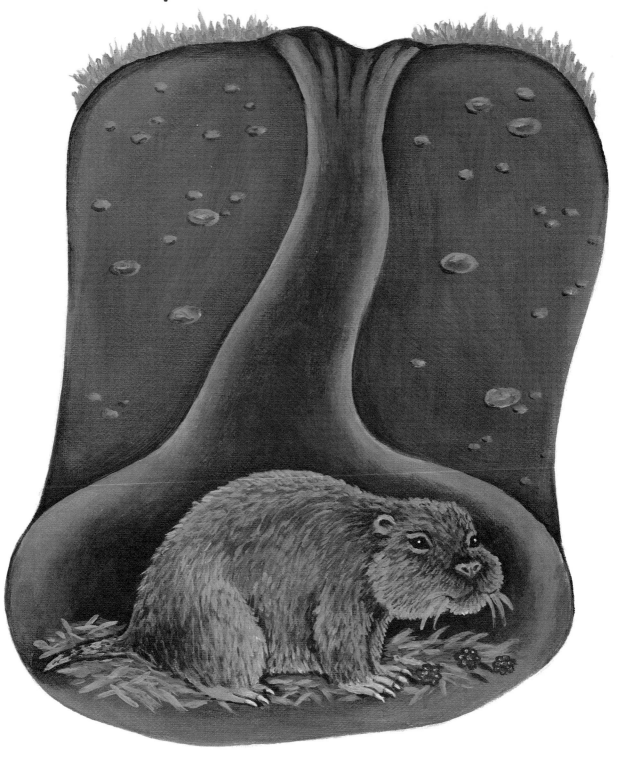

**A cougar and its kittens
were sleeping in the sun.
They think that night's a better time
to pounce and hunt and run.**

Then my eagle friend said good-bye
and circled high above the land.
When I awoke I saw it
in the picture in my hand!